Stories of Magic Ponies

Susanna Davidson

Illustrated by Jana Costa

Reading Consultant: Alison Kelly
Roehampton University

Map of Pony Island

Coco's house

Star's house

Meadows

Beauty Contest Area

Royal Palace

Contents

Chapter 1

The Beauty Contest

Pony Island was buzzing with excitement. The Beauty Contest was in three days' time and every pony wanted to win.

"I'm sure I'll be the winner," said Star. "I'm *so* beautiful."

"But it's not just about beauty," said Speckle. "You have to be the best-dressed pony too."

"It makes it much harder not being allowed to use magic to make our outfits," Coco added.

"It doesn't bother me," said Star. "After all, I won last year *and* the year before."

"So you did," said Speckle, with a sigh.

"I wish I could win," whispered Coco. "Just once."

"Dream on," snorted Star.
"It's never going to happen."

All the ponies worked hard,
getting their outfits ready.
Coco worked hardest of all.

She stayed up all night,
making a wonderful cloak of
silver, gold and sparkling stars.

But Star was spying on her.
"Coco's cloak is better than
mine," she realized. "I *can't* let
her win."

On the day of the contest, Star waited until Coco trotted off to the Pony Pools for a swim. Then she sneaked into her house and cast a spell on the cloak.

"Oh no!" cried Coco, when she came back. "My cloak's ruined. And there's no time to make a new one."

Coco cantered straight out of her house and down to the meadows. It was so pretty there, it usually cheered her up.

But not this time. Coco sank down under a rose bush and cried herself to sleep.

She slept until the sun set in the sky.

Turning her head, Coco saw that rose petals had fallen on her back and a butterfly was resting in her mane. Suddenly, she had a wonderful idea.

At the Beauty Contest, the Pony Queen was about to announce the winner. Star was sure she'd win.

Beauty contest

"We should wait for Coco," said the Pony Queen.
"She's not coming," Star put in quickly.

14

"Oh yes she is," said Speckle. All the ponies turned. There stood Coco...

Her mane was thick with rose petals. Butterflies danced over her back and a garland of flowers hung from her neck.

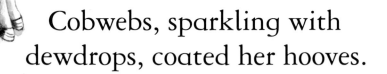

Cobwebs, sparkling with dewdrops, coated her hooves.

The Pony Queen trotted straight up to Coco. She placed the Beauty Contest crown over her ears.

"Coco is this year's winner!" she declared.

"Neigh! Neigh! Neigh!"
cheered the ponies.

Coco had never felt happier.

Star was furious. "Coco's
won the contest," she moaned,
"and *I* helped her win it!"

Chapter 2

Moonbeam in a mess

"It's not fair," said Moonbeam, stamping her hooves. "All the other ponies have beautiful coats and I'm plain white."

"Your coat *is* beautiful. It glows like the moon," said her mother. "Besides, you can't change the way you are."

"I'm not giving up that easily," thought Moonbeam. "Maybe Shadow can help me."

Shadow was the most magical pony on the island. But ponies said her magic was as dark as her name.

The next morning, Moonbeam trotted through the Dark Woods to Shadow's house.

"Can you help me?" she asked. "I want an amazing coat. I want to be peachy pink or fiery red. Just not white!"

"Hmm," said Shadow, thoughtfully. "Perhaps I can help." She picked up a brush and began to paint Moonbeam's coat with magic glue.

"Now fly to the rainbow," said Shadow. "Whatever shade you fly through will stick to your coat."

"But only fly through one band in the rainbow," Shadow added.

"I promise," said Moonbeam, fluttering her wings. She flew higher and higher, until she reached the rainbow.

But when Moonbeam saw
the rose reds and shining
purples, the bright greens and
golden yellows, she wanted
them *all* on her coat.

Ignoring Shadow's warning,
Moonbeam weaved in and out
of the rainbow. She painted her
coat with all its shades.

Then she flew down to the
Pony Pools, to show off to
all the other ponies.

"Look at me!" she called.

Everyone was silent. Then her mother gasped. "Oh Moonbeam!" she cried. "What have you done?"

Moonbeam looked at her legs and her back. All the shades had mixed together to make a horrible, murky mess.

27

"Oh no! I'm ruined!"
neighed Moonbeam.

"I thought this might
happen," said Shadow, trotting
out from behind a tree.

Moonbeam blushed.
"So," Shadow went on,
"I didn't use waterproof glue.
Splash her everyone!"

All the
ponies splashed
Moonbeam until
she was sopping wet.

"Stop!" whinnied Moonbeam, until she saw the water was washing away the rainbow.

"I look like me again!" she cried. "And I want to stay that way."

Chapter 3

Bluebell's spell

Bluebell the unicorn was about to cast her first spell. She lowered her head, aimed her horn and...

"Wait!" neighed Shadow, her magic teacher. "What are you doing?"

"I'm going to cast my first spell," said Bluebell, proudly, "and turn this frog into a stone."

"Remember the magic rules," said Shadow. "Never cast a spell unless you know how to undo it."

"Oh yes," said Bluebell. She paused. "Um... how do you undo this one again?"

"Try to work it out for yourself," said Shadow. "If you can't, I'll tell you next lesson."

"In the meantime, leave that frog alone."

34

Bluebell was still staring at
the frog when her friend, Puck,
came up to her. "What are
you doing?" Puck asked.

"I'm about to cast my first
spell..." Bluebell began.

"Ooh! Go on!" said Puck.
"The spell can't be *that* hard
to undo," thought Bluebell.
"Now where's the frog gone..."

Bluebell aimed her horn at the
frog, took a deep breath and
shouted, *"Kazaam Kazaar!"*

There was a flash and a
bang and suddenly instead of
the frog there was... a stone.

"Ribbit," said the stone.

"Wow!" said Puck. "That's amazing. Now let's see you turn it back again."

"Yes," said Bluebell. "Er..."

"You do know how, don't you?" asked Puck, worriedly.

"Of course," said Bluebell. She pointed her horn at the stone and once again cried out, "*Kazaam Kazaar!*"

There was a flash and a
bang and suddenly instead
of the stone there was...
a caterpillar.

"Ribbit!" said the caterpillar.

40

"Bluebell!" said Puck. "You don't know how to undo the spell, do you? Shadow will be furious."

"I can undo it," said Bluebell, trying again. But each time she cast her spell, it went wrong...

"Oh no," sobbed Bluebell,
tears dripping down her nose.

"I have an idea," said Puck.
"Say the spell in reverse."

"In reverse?" asked Bluebell.
"Oh, I see... *Raazak Maazak!*"
she chanted.

BANG went the bird and...
"The frog's back!" cried Puck.

"Hooray!" neighed Puck and
Bluebell together.

"What a relief," added
Bluebell. "Now Shadow need
never know..."

"Oh really?" said the frog.
Bluebell and Puck looked at
each other, then at the frog.

BANG went the frog and, in a flash, there stood Shadow.

"It was you all along?" gasped Bluebell.

"It was," said Shadow. "I had a feeling you wouldn't leave that frog alone."

46

"I'm sorry," said Bluebell, hanging her head in shame.

"Never mind," said Shadow, laughing. "I think you've learned your lesson now."

Series editor: Lesley Sims

Designed by
Katarina Dragoslavic
and Louise Flutter

First published in 2007 by Usborne Publishing Ltd., Usborne House,
83-85 Saffron Hill, London EC1N 8RT, England. www.usborne.com
Copyright © 2007 Usborne Publishing Ltd.